George Henry Borrow, Johannes Ewald

The Death of Balder

George Henry Borrow, Johannes Ewald

The Death of Balder

ISBN/EAN: 9783337387938

Printed in Europe, USA, Canada, Australia, Japan

Cover: Foto ©Andreas Hilbeck / pixelio.de

More available books at **www.hansebooks.com**

THE
DEATH OF BALDER

FROM THE DANISH

OF

JOHANNES EWALD

(1773)

TRANSLATED BY

GEORGE BORROW

AUTHOR OF "BIBLE IN SPAIN," "LAVENGRO," "WILD WALES," ETC.

LONDON
JARROLD & SONS, 3 PATERNOSTER BUILDINGS, E.C.

1889

PREFACE TO THE TRANSLATION.

THE works of the late poet Ewald are deservedly popular in Denmark. The present tragedy, and the opera of "The Fishermen" ("Fiskerne"), in which occurs the bold lyric which has become the national song of the Danes, are esteemed his best productions.

For the fidelity with which the present version has been made I appeal to those of my countrymen who understand the original, and demand whether I have given a thought or expression equivalents to which are not to be found in the Danish tragedy.

I have imitated the peculiar species of blank verse in which the original is composed, in order that the English reader may form an exact idea thereof, and though by having done so my poetry may have somewhat of a cramped, embarrassed gait, I have a firm hope that I shall not meet very severe reprehension for having sacrificed elegance to fidelity.

GEORGE BORROW.

THE PERSONS.

BALDER.	HOTHER.
THOR.	NANNA.
LOKE.	THE THREE VALKYRIER.

The place of action is a pine-wood on the Norwegian mountains. Round about it are seen steep and uneven rocks. The top of the hindermost and highest is covered with snow.

THE

DEATH OF BALDER.

———•—•—

ACT THE FIRST.

*BALDER and THOR are seated upon stones at some distance
from each other. Both are armed—THOR with his
hammer, and BALDER with spear and sword.*

BALDER. Land whose proud and rocky bosom
Braves the sky continually !

THOR. Where should strength and valour blossom,
Land of rocks, if not in thee ?

BALDER. Odin's shafts of ruddy levin
Back from thy hard sides are driven ;
Never sun thy snow dispels.

THOR. Sure, he'll joy in deeds of daring,
Ne'er for ease voluptuous caring,
Who upon the mountain dwells.

BOTH. Land whose proud and rocky bosom
Braves the sky continually !
Where should strength and valour blossom,
Land of rocks, if not in thee ?

B

BALDER (*he springs up, but* THOR *remains sitting, like
one in deep thought*).   Ha ! I will quickly fly from thee
for ever,

Thou hated land, where everything so proudly
Upbraids me for my weakness—for my fetters :
Where I, pursu'd by pains of hopeless passion,
The live-long nights among deaf rocks do wander—
Whose echoes sport with Balder's lamentations,
Each cold, each feelingless, as Nanna's bosom,
The fair, unpitying savage !

THOR.   Son of Odin !

BALDER. Speak, mighty Thor !

THOR.   Thou sighest, then—and
vainly ?

BALDER. Vainly : without a glimpse of hope ; bewildered.
What, what have I not promised, vow'd, attempted ?
How oft have I, O Thor !—I blush, but hear it—
To tears debas'd myself : my tears have trickled—
Have vainly trickled—before Gevar's daughter.

THOR. Ha ! Gevar's daughter ?

BALDER.   Yes, the haughty Nanna.

THOR. Dost   mean   the   daughter   of   the   wise   King
Gevar,

Who reads the actions of the unborn hero,
The will of Fate, malicious foemen's projects,
And war and death of warriors in the planets :
Dost mean his daughter ?

BALDER. Think'st thou other fathers possess a Nanna?

THOR. Gods!

[*He again casts his eyes upon the ground, like one
who meditates deeply.*

BALDER. Behind yon pine wood he built an altar unto
    thee and Odin,
There thou mayst see the roof of his still dwelling.
There lives the earthly Freia—cruel maiden—
There slumbers she, perhaps—the proud one rests in
Joy's downy arms, undreaming aught of Balder!
As if I did not love, were not a half-god;
As if by Skalds my name were never chanted
As if I were a demon, bad as Loke!
Ha! if upon my tongue lurked bane and magic,
When fear enchains it and the pale lip trembles;
When broken words and a disordered wailing
Are all with which I can express my bosom's
Desire intense, and dread unwonted torments.
Ha! were my voice like Find's when he, distracted,
Goes over Horthedal; as when he bellows,
And wild at last, and blind with fury, splinters
The oaks, the glory of the sacred forest.
Ha! if the blood of maids and unarm'd wretches
Of harmless travellers, stained the hands of Balder—
If ruddy lightnings burnt between these fingers—

Then might'st thou well be pale;
And thou wert right to fly from me, O Nanna!

THOR. Now, Balder, hear my word, and fly from Nanna!

BALDER. From Nanna! Yes, I ought—that see I plainly.
Ha! some accursed fiend my foot has fasten'd
To these wild mountains and to Nanna's shadow!
And is there nothing then of hope remaining?
When did I first become so grim—so frightful?
When? Tell me, Thor, is breath of mine destructive?
Has death among my tears and smiles its dwelling?
What shall I do? Reply! But thou art silent,
And from thine eyeball flames contemptuous anger.

THOR (*he rises*). Ha! drivellest thou before the God of
    Thunder?

BALDER. To Thor, to Odin's friend, I breathe my sorrow.

THOR. How long dost think, degenerate son of Odin,
Unmanly pining for a foolish maiden,
And all the weary train of love-sick follies,
Will move a bosom that is steeled by virtue?
Thou dotest! Dote and weep, in tears swim ever;
But by thy father's arm, by Odin's honour,
Haste, hide thy tears and thee in shades of alder!
Haste to the still, the peace-accustom'd valley,
Where lazy herdsmen dance amid the clover.
There wet each leaf which soft the west wind kisses,
Each plant which breathes around voluptuous odours,
With tears! There sigh and moan and the tired peasant

Shall hear thee, and, behind his ploughshare resting,
Shall wonder at thy grief, and pity Balder!

BALDER. And is this all the comfort thou canst offer?

THOR. I gave thee counsel: fly from her who flies thee!
What holds thee here, where thou canst hope for nothing?

BALDER. And can I? Ah, my friend, that is my duty!
But fly! And never, never see thee, Nanna!
And ne'er again behold the roof where under
Thou sleepest! Honour the mere thought destroyeth!
Ere that, I'll perish here, unfamed, forgotten!

THOR. Well, perish, then! I see too plain 'tis useless
Against a harsh, eternal fate to struggle!

      The hill fiend dreads my hammer's might

      Before it turns the Jotun white,

      And rocks, whereon I strike, give way.

      But nothing cruel fate can move;

      And what Allfather there above

      Resolves upon, stands firm for aye.

Know, son of Odin, thou whom reason, friendship,
Whom scorn—e'en scorn—to move are all unable,
Know that prophetic were thy words! Fate hastens!
The Valkyrie prepares the spear already,
Its deadly point already does she sharpen.
Ah, see! the prince of battle holds it brandish'd;
He strikes! he strikes! and all the Aser sorrow.

BALDER. Dark is thy speech, O Thor! dark as thy visage.

THOR. Before my eyes are murky shadows flitting.

A mortal youth, with blood of Asa crimson'd!
The fight and death of gods, the fall of Asgara!
Hear, son of Odin, wretched slave of passion,
Think not that dreams, that magic's foul deception,
That spectres of the night my brain bewilder;
And oh! think not that merely chance has led me
To Balder's presence, and to these high forests!
I sought thee, came with speed to give thee warning:
Fear, then! It is thy friend, 'tis Thor, who's speaking!
And on my lips I bear the words of Odin.
Thou know'st there grows in night's mysterious valley
A tree, as yet by men or gods seen never;
It bears a bough, which bough, when once 'tis harden'd
In Nastroud's flames, can slay thee.

  BALDER.   Yes, I know it.

  THOR. That knowest thou, friend! And is it a mere
    slumber,
A fleeting trance, a pleasant dream of battle,
With which the spear's impregnated in Nastroud?
Ha! whom it slays wakes never up in Valhall;
In mist and darkness must he lie for ever.
From gods and men alike for ever parted,
Must Balder be detested—Hæla's booty,
Not Odin's quest?

  BALDER.   Aye; when the tree's discover'd.

  THOR. Well, now, attend and heed a father's warning!
When Odin high from Lidskialf saw thee raving,

In toils of love, 'mong Norway's snowy mountains,
The speech of Mimmer on his heart fell heavy.
Hear it and tremble! Not for death, O Balder!
Nor e'en for Hæla, but thy father's anguish;
"The year"—such was his word (thou knowest Mimmer,
And scarce canst think he'd breathe the words of falsehood)—
"The year when Norway's desert hills shall echo
The half-god's wasted love-caus'd lamentations,
When he's rejected by a prophet's daughter,
That year shall see the spear which holds his ruin,
Shall see the gods in grief, and Odin weeping."
Hear that and quake! And fly, and spare thy father!
If not, dote on and die, for that's thy fortune!

       [He disappears among the trees.

  BALDER (*alone*). And must I die? Ah well, I merely
    forfeit
A worthless breath, which is by Nanna hated.
Ha! hated. How that thought that Nanna hates me
Torments my breast! Death, only death, can drown it.
It burns, it scorches me, like Nastroud's blazes.
Come, tenfold death, come quickly, and extinguish
The thought: destroy it, crush it, with this bosom.
Thanks be to Thor, for he my eyelids lifted,
Disclosing I had chance of rest—of dying!
E'en Surtur, he whose hostile fingers planted
The tree, the black tree, by the feeble starlight;
Who nurs'd its infant root with blood fresh taken

From slaughter'd babes, and drew a circle round it,
And mutter'd magic words, and gave it power
To shoot the bane of Nastroud in my bosom,
Was not so cruel as thyself, O Nanna!
What! cruel? No, by Odin! Pity drove him
To rear up remedy benign and grateful
For the dire wound with which thou torment'st me.
Ah, maid! thou mak'st me look to death with longing
And yet to die! and die from thee! and never——
Ha! my heart freezes! The mere word would kill me!
But then, most likely thou wilt pity Balder,
And with a hot, a precious tear bedew him!

> Say, O maid! when thou dost pour
> From thine eyes the briny shower
> O'er a lifeless lump of clay!
> Cease thy weeping, cruel maiden:
> All thy grief is vainly vented:
> See the breast so long tormented
> Which thy pity now should gladden,
> Beats no more and rots away!
> O Nanna! Nanna!

> > [*He sits down and holds both his hands
> > before his eyes.*

Loke (*in the shape of an old Finman*). Balder!

> > [*He walks in a crooked attitude, and supports him-
> > self upon a knotted staff. He enters so that his
> > back is turned to* Balder.

Help, ye gods of heaven !
Oh, I unfortunate ! that frost and hunger,
And fear of bears and wolves and evil spirits
Should now destroy me on these frightful mountains !
Oh, that I but beheld a smoke uprising,
A single trace of a bewildered hunter !
That I but heard a cheery horn resounding !
But nothing, nothing ! Never, never rises
A friendly sound among these wildernesses,
Which human feet till now has never trodden.
Ah ! who will succour me ?

BALDER (*goes towards him and takes him kindly by the
arm*). What ails thee, father ?

LOKE (*as if terrified*). Aha ! I can no more ! Ah !

BALDER. Come and rest thee !
Here lean upon my arm !

LOKE. Ah !

BALDER. How thou tremblest,
My hoary friend ! But cast thy terrors from thee—
There thou art safe : this breast is warmed by pity.

LOKE. Forgive me, sir ; forsooth, I was confounded !
Thou see'st in me a poor and ancient Finman.
Far, far away from these terrific mountains,
This year I built of flags and stones my hovel ;
I sought for reindeer—all my wealth ; they doubtless
Were captured by the bear ! I, wretched being !

My sight is feeble, and the night surprised me;
The wind, as I observe too late, has shifted,
And not a star is gleaming in the heavens:
Ah! far must be the way unto my hovel!
My feet are wearied out, for I have wandered
The long and chilly night among the mountains.

    BALDER. What wishest thou?

    LOKE.   I die of frost and hunger.
Whoe'er thou art, and if thou feelest pity—
Excuse my doubt—yet wouldst thou save the remnant
Of life which trembles on my lips, conduct me
Straight to the cheering hearth where bask thy servants.

    BALDER. The way would prove for thee too far; but
        see'st thou
The lofty roof behind the forest yonder,
There, there resides of earth the fairest daughter:
Thither repair, thou fortunate old stranger!
There she resides.—Ah! thou wilt be to Nanna
A dear, a welcome guest! She loves the wretched;
Her noble heart swells always with compassion
For every sufferer. Only not—— Thou stayest!
Why go'st thou not?

    LOKE.   I go; but thou wast speaking,
Methinks, of Nanna?

    BALDER.   Yes.

    LOKE.   Of Gevar's daughter?

    BALDER (*astonished*). Thou know'st her?

LOKE.   No; but oftentimes her bridegroom
Has come fatigued with hunting, to my hovel.

BALDER. Ah who—

LOKE (*turns away as if to depart*). She dwells there,
    does she?

BALDER (*seizes him by the arm*). Stay! who is the bride-
    groom?
Speak, reptile, speak! Who? When? Reply, thou traitor,
Or here thou diest!

LOKE.   Spare me, sir, in mercy!
I faint with terror!

BALDER.   Speak! by all the powers,
Thy smallest hair is sacred! I have promised.
Now, speak!

LOKE.   I am an old and harmless creature.

BALDER. But Nanna's bridegroom?   ·

LOKE.   Truly, sir, I wonder,
That one like thee, a dweller 'mongst these mountains,
Should know him not, the noblest and the bravest
Of all the sons of earth.

BALDER.   Ye gods of heaven!
And who? His name?

LOKE.   One who is bold as Odin,
And strong as Thor, and beautiful as Balder.

BALDER. Ha! kill me not, but answer: name him.

LOKE (*with a loud voice*).   Hother!

BALDER (*with agitation*). What! Who? The Leire King?
    The Skioldung Hother?

LOKE. Who here is foster'd up by Nanna's father.

BALDER. Thou killest me! Thou see'st how I tremble!
Yet, that I never saw him here! Where is he?

LOKE. At Gevar's.

BALDER.   By the gods, it overcomes me!
What, under Nanna's roof?

LOKE.   At night-time only,
As I believe; for ere the east hills redden,
Upstarts he, lovely as a young spring morning,
And griping firm his lusty spear, he wanders
Among the rocks. Ah, master! thou hast seen him—
Withouten doubt thou hast. 'Tis true he hideth
For some time past his god-like form in wadmal,*
And rolls beneath a rugged cap his tresses—
I wonder, wherefore.

BALDER.   Ha! thou flash of lightning,
Which clear'st all up at once! I, wretched madman!
How senseless was I, and by pride how blinded
To sons of earth my eyes I never lower'd.
Ah! is my proud solicitude thus baffled?
But she can only love the gods, I'm certain!

LOKE. Excuse me, sir, I do not understand thee.
She loves not Odin half so much as Hother.

BALDER. Fly, slave—begone! for Udgaard, Loke's poison,
Is on thy tongue! That foe of gods has sent thee:
Thou art his messenger, thou art—thou art, thou traitor! .

* Wadmal, a coarse woollen stuff, much worn by Norwegian peasants.

Dost dare to linger ?   But thou art in safety,
For, worm, thy weakness and my oath protect thee.
Ha ! I myself will fly before my fury.   [*He goes.*

LOKE (*he looks contemptuously after* BALDER, *then raises
    himself to his full height, discards at once his assumed
    figure, and appears as* LOKE). My weakness, mighty
    Balder ?   Do not scorn it !
To dust and ashes, boaster, it shall crush thee.
Not Loke's messenger, but Loke, stung thee.
Already bellows the young god with torment :
Hear, Odin ! hear thy lov'd one, hear him howling !
Delay thee not ! enjoy his voice and feel it !
Harmonious is it to the ears of Loke.
Quick, quick ! thou ne'er again, perchance, will hear it.
Survey him near : how swells each vein with poison,
Which I have poured into his breast with cunning !
Soon Odin, soon will thy beloved be silent ;
Soon from thy sight will Balder flit for ever ;
Then will it be thy turn to mourn, O tyrant !
It comes—the long-protracted day of vengeance !
It comes—the sigh'd-for hour of retribution !
How long hast thou not tortur'd Loke's bowels,
And fearless trampled 'neath thy feet his offspring ?
Hear Hæl and Fenris' Wolf, and Midgaard's Serpent—
Loud howl they !—hear them night and day proclaiming
Thy unmatched cruelty with frightful voices !

Each of them was a god, and fair as Balder,
But now to earth and heaven, and to myself, a horror :
Each is a monster, bow'd with chains of darkness.
The hour's at hand, the tardy hour of vengeance :
Already blow I in war's horn : to combat,
Up, up ye mighty gods, and rescue Balder !
There see I him, the hero youth, who only,
Arm'd with the tree of death by Odin's maidens,
Can be—so Fate decrees—this Balder's slayer.
And he shall be it : quickly shall he brandish
The life-destroying bough, if Asa Loke,
By mighty art and wonderful delusions,
Knows how to work the maidens to his purpose.
He comes !   I will conceal myself, and listen.

HOTHER, *and presently* LOKE—*the first dressed like a
    Norwegian peasant, with a hunting-spear in his hand ;
    the other undistinguished.*

HOTHER (*he comes down from the rocks and unbinds the
skiers* * *from his feet ere he steps forward on the scene*).
                 Upon the oak's summit,
                 A squirrel at play
                 Deceives with a rustle
                 The hunter so gay ;

---

    * Skiers are wooden pattens to run upon over the frozen snow.

He starts, and, low crouching,
 His spear he grasps tight,
And, swelling up, boundeth
 His hand with delight.

Now quick—be not daunted !
 He's coming—take heed !
The bold bear, the old bear,
 Doth hitherward speed.
Oh, sound the most pleasant
 This ear ever knew !
He cometh—a bigger
 This weapon ne'er slew.

Thou sovereign of forests !
 Thou pride of thy race !
Oh, fortunate hunter—
 Oh, glorious chase !
Now quick ! be not daunted,
 He comes—be prepared !
Where is he, the savage ?
 His bellow, who heard ?

No more on the oak-top
 The squirrel doth play ;
Deceived has a rustle
 The hunter so gay ;

No sound as he listens
　　His hearing assails,
Save the pattering of leaves
　　That are moved by the gales.

There comes he—where?　Oh, what a foolish stripling
Am I, who here about four days have wandered
In quest of a mere phantom!　Surely, Nanna,
Thou dost deceive me—dost but prove thy lover ;
And think'st thou, virtuous one, that if a godhead
Came down in light effulgent, and before thee
Knelt and laid heaven at thy feet—Ha! think'st
Thou that fear, base doubt of Nanna's faith and
Honour, would sully Hother's breast?　I know thou
Lovest me—thou hast avowed it : what shall then
This wooer avail—this wooer who must not be
Anger'd?　Why the deception?

　　LOKE.　　　　　　　　　Hail, thou son of Hothbrod!

　　HOTHER (*astonished*). Ha! scarcely do I know myself!
　　　By Odin,
I look more like a rugged elf than Hother.
And who art thou, that knowest me? who art thou?

　　LOKE. My name is Vanfred!　When thy mother bore thee
I was at hand and swore unto thee friendship.

　　HOTHER. Grim　is　thy　visage,　and　thine　eye　doth
　　　promise,
But little good.　What dost thou seek?

LOKE.   Whom, Skolding,
Whom fearest thou ?   Why hide in yonder vestments ?
   HOTHER. I fear ? thou warlock ! Wise thou wert in
      speaking
Of friendship !
   LOKE.   Spare thy wrath my youthful warrior !
Reserve it for thy foes !
   HOTHER.   They shall not miss it !
   LOKE. And yet 'tis plain thou hidest thee from some one.
   HOTHER. It was Nanna bade me. Ha ! I blush by
      heaven !
When Nanna spake I always blindly listen'd.
She has disguised me, as thou see'st, stranger ;
She plagues me with her fears ; the dreamer would
      not—
Would really not—for all the wide world's riches,
That the wood goblin, or perhaps some lover
Invisible, should know me.
   LOKE.   Pretty folly !
Balder invisible ! the handsome half-god !
   HOTHER. What ! Balder, son of Odin ?   He her lover ?
O heaven !   Say, where is he ? where ?
   LOKE.   With Nanna.
   HOTHER. There ?   Now ? (*After some reflection.*) She
      drove me out.
   LOLE.   Perhaps, thou see'st
That she has rid herself of thee by cunning,

                                            c

HOTHER. I simply thought the Alf had caus'd thy terror;
But Balder, false one, he shall soon experience
That I fear no one.   [*About to go.*

LOKE.   Softly, prince! be cautious!
I see thy courage; but thy foe is mighty.

HOTHER. Is my arm weak?

LOKE.   It is against a half-god;
Yet he can die. I know a spear which slayeth.

HOTHER. Thou dreamest!

LOKE.   Spare thy doubts. That spear or nothing
Can wound his breast.—But see, the sun is rising,
And I must fly to subterranean places;
But I'll forsake thee not. This horn I give thee,
And when thy need is greatest, then, O Hother!
Blow strongly in that horn, and turning westward,
Call thrice aloud on Vanfred—Vanfred! Vanfred!

> [*The two last times he cries it with a hollow voice,
> after having disappeared among the rocks, and
> the last time of all evidently farther away than
> the other. Immediately thereupon a noise is
> heard among the rocks, as of distant thunder.*

HOTHER, *and presently* NANNA.

HOTHER (*casts away the horn*). Accurs'd be thou, thy
    horn, and all thy magic!
Is Hother fearful? Does he crave in battle

The aid of warlocks and of arts ignoble ?
Is not my arm sufficient ?   Ha ! I'll show thee !

> [*He is going ; but* NANNA *meets him at the entrance of
> the scene.*

NANNA. Where now ?
HOTHER.   I go to dare the wrath of Balder.
NANNA. (*affrighted*). Ah !
HOTHER.   His stern look may teach me how to tremble.
NANNA. O Heaven !
HOTHER.   Hold me not !
NANNA (*anxiously and affectionately*). Where now, my
    Hother ?
HOTHER. I soon shall find him !

> [*He goes in spite of* NANNA's *endeavour to detain him.*

NANNA.   Ah ! he goes—he rages ;
And Balder yells with wrath.   Some serpent surely
Has breath'd to-day his poison in their bosoms.
They hate, they seek each other !   Who asunder
Will hold the raging bears.   Ah ! who will soften
The foaming ones ?   I have this hour expected,
And long by art have I delay'd its coming ;
But now is art, and prayer, and all else useless :
E'en now they meet in conflict.   I am powerless !
What can my tears avail ?   Alas ! blood only
Will satiate them and Heaven : thine must trickle,
My Hother.   What art thou against a half-god ?

When thy fire, Ourath, but glimmers,
Tears can quench it instantly;
But it flames, and now 'twere wonder
Could the weak drops keep it under.
Ah! thy blazes fierce and cruel
In the lov'd one's grief find fuel,
And are fann'd by plaintive cry.
Tear, with which mine eye is swelling,
Thou canst not remove the ill;
O keep in thou fruitless wailing,
Let my bosom hide thee still.   [*She goes.*

ACT THE SECOND.

The three VALKRIER. *They are armed as war-maids, and besides the spears which hang over their shoulders, each has a short spear in her hand: they take each other by the hands, and walk in a circle, singing.*

All three.   O'er the hill, o'er the dell,
O'er the sea's foamy waters,
Unweariedly ply,
Valhalla, thy daughters,
The blood-dropping wing:
Die, battle, and die!
Is the bidding they bring.

The first.   Not fever's foul pains.
The second.   Not hunger.

The third.	Not chains.
All three.	But fight and delight.
	For the brave ever brings,
	Valhalla, thy daughters,
	By light and by night,
	O'er the land and the waters,
	With blood-drooping wing.
The first.	The crash of the spear,
	In deadly career,
	Is alone to me dear.
The second.	The feeble moan press'd
	From the dying man's breast
	Is what pleases me best.
The third.	The cry on the plain
	Round the corse of the slain
	I list to most pain.
All three.	Die, battle, and die !
	O'er the hill, o'er the dell,
	O'er the sea's foamy waters,
	Unweariedly ply,
	Valhalla, thy daughters,
	The blood-dropping wing :
	Die, battle, and die,
	Is the bidding they bring.

The first. I hear the sound of arms; but now it ceases.
How long will he delay, the noble warrior?

The second. Whom wait'st thou for?

The first.   And thou? what will my sister
In this wild spot which blood has never crimson'd?

   The second. What has assembled us? and here where
     scarcely
A sword has flashed since days of Jotun Ymer,
Was it a god or destiny which drove us?

   The first. Thou knowest that the morning sun illumines
Ten thousand spears on Scotland's heathy mountains;
High beats with joy each warrior's heart.   In silence,
They forward press, and only wait my on-cry.
Thither would I—but hear the strange adventure
Which stopp'd my flight upon these rocks.   Envelop'd
In a black, tempest, I a Finman follow'd,
Who boldly climb'd the mountain summits,
And sprang o'er every yawning rift undaunted:
Then saw I Hothbrod's valiant son.   I saw him
As in the brook he cleans from dust his armour,
And sharp'd laboriously his rusty dagger,
And prov'd upon the pine's thick stem his falchion;
Then brandish'd he his hunting-spear: far backward
He drew his nervous arm; I heard the weapon
Hiss, but my eye beheld it scarce a moment,
For like the lightning which the black clouds swallow
It vanished, and the heir vainly sought it.
Then look'd I round about, and saw my Finman,
Who held the spear and laugh'd; I storm'd with fury.
Then down he plung'd within a midnight chasm;

And from the deep uprose a voice like thunder
Which slowly booms among the Finnish deserts.
" Unarm'd," it bellow'd, "shall the warrior perish?
Wither shall he of age, and deep in Hælheim
Be hidden, far from Odin, far from Valhal."
Angry, I rooted up the oaks in search of
A spear for battle's friend—and this I fix'd on;
I gave it tempest's speed and strength to humble
Each warrior whom it smiteth, when with wonder
Of thy fast sounding voice I heard an echo.

    The second. Ye stars! what sorcery! But to me now
        listen!

I hasten'd unto Hortha's gloomy forests,
To glut myself in Roman blood; then look'd I
Down from the thunder-cloud in which I journey'd,
And on these towering hills my eyes I fastened;
Then saw I Denmark's Hother, prince of battle,
Like the rock-pine, which o'er the ocean beetles;
He stood, and storm-winds with his locks were playing,
Then from the brake a wolf sprang, grim and frightful,
And big as Fenri's Wolf: the Skoldung saw it,
And brandish'd high his spear.   Forth went it booming,
As booming goes from the cold North a whirlwind;
Straight vanished wolf and spear; but deep a-forest
Was heard as from a thousand wolves a howling.
" See, see," it howl'd, " the Skoldung Hother loses
His spear, and in his hand the sword is fragile.

Now have we peace, and Norway's Kemps may slumber."
Disturb'd at such dark sorcery, I seiz'd on
The spear of steel thou see'st, and laid lightning
And fiends' death on its point, when I beheld thee.

   The third (who hitherto has stood in deep thought). Sharp
      is my sight in war; but here is darkness.
But do not think that chance and magic
Here assembled battle's angry daughters.
Allfather for the fight prepares; Allfather
Assembles us with murky wink: I saw him,
The mighty Thor; wroth was he, and his hammer
Was in his hand.   He stood by Gevar's dwelling:
He spoke to me, and soon as e'er I answer'd
He vanished, thundering in the eastern heavens.
It is not sport, nor any childish quarrel,
Be ye assured, makes Thor descend from Asgaard.

   The first. He spake to thee?

   The third.   As when the warriors slumber,
And suddenly are wak'd to thousand dangers
By din of shields and mingled squadrons' tumult,
So tower'd he up and shouted when he saw me,
And dread and hollow as the ocean's bellow,
As moan of forests in the nightly tempest,
Sounded his voice unto my ear!
" What, Rota!" he shouted; Rota here! "Ye gods of heaven!
Whom seekest thou, where unclomb rocks engirdle
Peace, smiling peace? O say! whom, sent by Skulda,

Wilt thou devote upon the stilly mountains ?
But ah ! what light had I the power to kindle ?
Dark is my spirit.   The terrific Norna,
She who allots to time, ere it approaches,
It's luck, and binds it with determined fingers
Unto Fate's will, is silent, and drives Rota
Far from each plain belov'd where battle rages.
Yet shook the fatal spear with which conflicting
Monarchs I greet, at sunrise thrice it trembled ;
And death lies heavy in my arm—that know I,
But for the victim.

    The first.   Threatens Fate our Hother ?

    The second. Thor's fear and even thine betoken danger.

    The third. So seems it. Ah ! if it concern'd our Hother !
Ye mind full well how high the Danish hero
I ever lov'd—I saw him by a fountain,
Dejected, weaponless, and half in slumber ;
But deep into the forest fled the savage,
From whom he took his sword, the sharp-edged Mimer,
And Hother's spear in his rude hands he carried.
" Retain my falchion, thou ferocious warrior !
Little in conflict shall it e'er avail thee !"
So shouted he, and all the rocks resounded.
Then straight I brought my choicest spear from Valhall—
Long since I cut it from a lonely wild beech,
Which, hid from day, grew up in Lapland's deserts ;
A circle of grey stones stood round about it,

On each was clotted blood, and bones, and ashes ;
Blood as I cut the spear the stem emitted—
It crushes stone, and steel, and giants' armour.

HOTHER, THE OTHERS.

HOTHER (*he is armed, but without a spear*).   Where is
this prince of beauty, Nanna's half-god ?
> [*He starts slightly upon perceiving the* VALKYRIER.
> *They advance towards him, hand in hand.*

Excuse me my astonishment, fair war-maids !

The first. Hail to thee dauntless warrior, bane of Gelder !

The second. Hail to thee, Skoldung, valiant son of Hothbrod !

The third. Hail, hail to thee, my Hother, Leire's ruler !

HOTHER (*astonished.*)   Ye know me !

The third.   Yes, thou noble youth, and love thee !

HOTHER. Your goodness overwhelms me—to what godhead

Stand I indebted for this lucky meeting ?

The first. I bring to thee a spear to fight with heroes !

The second. And this, I hand to thee, can slaughter
demons !

The third. This spear is excellent in fight with Jotuns.

HOTHER. How shall I e'er repay these costly presents ?

The first. Be valiant! fight! send battle's sons to Valhall !

The second. Extend the Danish sway and Odin's worship !

The third. The sire of many warlike kings of Leire !

> [*They vanish.*

HOTHER. There's nought but sorcery upon these mountains!

They've vanished!   Do I dream to-day?   Where am I?

Sight, feeling, reason are alike enchanted!

But here, ye gods! here in my bosom rages

The magic—Vanfred's poison.   Nanna, Nanna!

Shall I mistrust thee, then—shall I, thy Hother?

> [*He places the two spears against a tree, whereon he
> hangs his shield. That which the first* VALKYRIER
> *gave him he retains in his hand.*

The fire which love enkindles
  First warms with bliss the heart,
But soon, ah! soon the traitor
  Awaketh burning smart!
Love's flame at first discloses
  Pure innocence alone ;
But quickly by its splendour
  A deed of guilt is shown.
O love! thy bliss is vanish'd,
Thy flame extinguish quite,
For in my bride black falsehood
Now only meets my sight.

NANNA, HOTHER.

NANNA (*who has stood at the entrance of the scene, and
  has heard the latter part of* HOTHER'S *song*).   I
  overheard thee, weak, ignoble Hother!

HOTHER. Ah yes, weak! credulous!

NANNA. Save thyself repentance!

HOTHER. Where is thy demigod?

NANNA. This bosom, Hother, acquitteth me;
That were enough for Nanna, if——

HOTHER. Oh, pray, proceed!

NANNA (*affectionately*). Lov'd less——

HOTHER (*contemptuously*). Whom? Balder?

NANNA. Savage! what fiend has pour'd into thy bosom
His bane of late? Ha! fly from me: detest me!
Wilt thou love her thou canst mistrust!

HOTHER.   Ah, Nanna!

NANNA. I have debas'd myself to excusation
(Virtue from that, O Hother, ever shrinketh);
Yet trust'st thou not?—one's wont to trust the lov'd one!
Thou know'st (I told it thee before) that Gevar,
Thy wise instructor, has declar'd that Heaven
Threatens a bloody, horrible misfortune,
In case our love be nois'd about in Asgaard,
Ere certain stars shall stand in other orbits;
And canst thou wonder when so great an Asa
As Odin's Balder cometh unexpected,
That I all trembling will conceal——

HOTHER.   Ha, trembling!
My curse upon the slave who first invented
A word which ne'er my Nanna's lips should sully;
Thy excusations kill me! I imagined

It was a chaste, a maidenish reflection,
That made my Nanna blush at our affection :
Unmurmuring I obeyed, and kept in secret.
Why hast thou ta'en from me that sweet delusion ?
Why spak'st thou not, and say for whom thou tremblest ?
For Balder's death ? Thou lovest then thy half-god.
But no, ye gods ! No, I believe thee, Nanna !
It is for mine, for Hother's death, thou fearest.
Then think'st thou me so weak, so wholly powerless,
And lov'st me still ? When e'er lov'd maids the dastard ?

NANNA. 'Tis no disgrace to quake before a half-god !

HOTHER. 'Fore Odin's self mere cowards quake. Now hear
I—I, or Balder, die to-day !   [me !

NANNA.   O Hother !
I came to quarrel, came prepar'd with anger;
But ah, in burning tears it soon has melted.
Thou die, or Balder ! he—a half-god !

HOTHER.   Nanna !
Thy tears insult me sore, and yet—I know not—
They gladden me—they torture—they enchant me.
I love them—I excuse them—I—I know not——
O tear—sweet, bitter tear, desist from flowing !
Thou showest tenderness—but ah ! betrayest
Mistrust and slight respect !—ah, love thy Hother,
But oh ! believe, he will deserve thee, Nanna :
Thy heart is far too noble for the coward
Who beareth shield and sword and yet can tremble.

HOTHER. The slave only feareth.

NANNA. The hero can fall!

HOTHER. Ah then his fame cheereth
His bride in her thrall.

NANNA. Ah then his bride weeps!

HOTHER. She's honour'd.

NANNA. She weepeth!

HOTHER. She's honour'd.

NANNA. And weepeth.

HOTHER. Ah, then his fame cheereth
His bride in her thrall.

Both. Ah then his fame cheereth
His bride in her thrall.

NANNA. Ah, if thou now fallest?

HOTHER. And if I now fall?

NANNA. Then I shall be wasted
By ne'er-ceasing smart.

HOTHER. But were my fame blasted
Then break would thy heart.

NANNA. Oh! what is remaining?

HOTHER. My valour's proud story.

NANNA. Mere grief and complaining!

HOTHER. My name is thy glory.

NANNA. Oh! if thou now fallest.

HOTHER. And if I now fall,

NANNA. Then I shall be wasted
With grief and complaining!

HOTHER. My name is remaining ;
　　　　　But honour once blasted
　　　　　We both should lose all.
Both.　　The slave only feareth,
　　　　　The hero can fall ;
　　　　　But then his fame cheereth
　　　　　His bride in her thrall.

NANNA (*with a terrified look, she seizes* HOTHER *by the arm,
upon perceiving* BALDER). Ah ! Hother, come.

BALDER, HOTHER, NANNA.

BALDER. Dost fly me, cruel Nanna !
Am I so frightful ? how have I offended ?
　　HOTHER (*will rush towards* BALDER, *but* NANNA *makes
　　every effort to prevent him*). Ha, Balder, we have
　　met at last.
NANNA (*much agitated*). My Hother !
Ah, if thou lovest me—if thou respectest my prayer——
　　BALDER. Thy Hother ?　O, ye gods ! how bitter !
　　HOTHER. To thee, perhaps to me 'tis sweet and grateful !
　　BALDER (*with majesty*). Presumptuous one !
　　NANNA (*casts herself in her anguish nearly at* HOTHER's
　　feet, who is about to lay hands on BALDER).　If thou
　　hast ever lov'd me,
Come with me, Hother ! come unto my father !
　　HOTHER. What ! shall I fly ?

NANNA.   Do thou whate'er thou pleasest !
Thou wouldst not have me perish in the forest,
Thou wouldst not, sure, that I should be a witness——
   BALDER. Ha, Nanna ! fly not from me !
   HOTHER (*to* BALDER).   Thou commandest,
I say she shall fly from thee. (*To* NANNA) Come, my
      Nanna !
(*To* BALDER). But do not thou despair ! nor yet imagine
Thou wilt have long to wait, if wait thou darest.

               [HOTHER *and* NANNA *exeunt.*

   BALDER. Ha ! wherefore crush'd I not to earth the
      brawler ?
But Nanna loves him—and shall Balder render
Nanna unhappy, cause despair to enter
Her breast, and dim with tears her eyes' effulgence ?
And what is his offence, the noble hero ?
He loves—ha, who can gaze upon thy beauties
And love thee not, proud maiden ?   But he braves me !
Ah ! he is young and fortunate, and if I
Had slain him now, 'twas Nanna's love I punish'd,
And not his insolence ; and, O my bosom !
Shall thy pure flame dishonour thee ?   No, Balder !
Love on and die, but of thyself be worthy !
Ha, let me lose my life and all, Allfather !
And Nanna e'en !   Yes, let me lose e'en Nanna !
But not the virtue she herself doth honour !

[*He hangs his shield upon a tree, which is opposite to
    that where* HOTHER's *hangs, and sets his spear up
    against it.*

True bliss, through virtue only known,
By virtue's self deserv'd alone.
Only for thee doth Balder sigh :
My sad heart would a heaven disdain
Which through dishonour it must gain.
So dear let slaves enjoyment buy !
Yes, Balder, worthy of thyself continue !
Canst thou wish Nanna to abandon Hother ?
Wish her whose virtue thy high soul so worships
Should weak and base become for thy advantage ?
But—does she love him ? has he won her promise ?
Who knoweth but she merely has dissembled,
And shown a fictious flame to prove thee, Balder !
Transporting dream !

NANNA, BALDER.

NANNA (*rushes in, terrified*). Ha ! Balder if thou
    lovest—— Ah, if thou——
BALDER (*casts himself at* NANNA's *feet*). Heavens,
    Nanna ! canst thou doubt it ?
I burn, I burn !

    [*Whilst* NANNA *in her terror makes every effort to
        raise him, they come into a familiar attitude, in
        which* HOTHER, *who has slain bears, and who is*

D

*wiping the blood from his spear at the moment
he appears, perceives them. He starts, and
remains standing among the trees, so that he
cannot hear what they say.*

NANNA.   Oh, rescue then my Hother!
Two savage bears among the bushes yonder
Attack'd him; if thou hast love for virtue,
Assist him quick; if thou delayest a moment,
The noblest heart that ever beat they'll mangle!
Oh! quick : bethink thee not!
  BALDER.   No, cruel Nanna!
Fear not!   My arm shall rescue him thou lovest!
   [*Just as he is about to rise* HOTHER *steps forward.*

HOTHER, THE LAST.

HOTHER. Ye heavens! do I dream? Enamour'd half-god!
Excuse me for disturbing thee!
  BALDER (*as he rises up*).   There is he!
  NANNA (*goes tenderly to meet* HOTHER). Ah, Hother! Ah,
   my Hother!
  HOTHER (*pushes her back with his hand*). Go, false
   woman!
  BALDER. Gods, how unthankful art thou—how ferocious!
Can such a bear of Nanna be deserving?
  HOTHER (*takes his shield down from the tree*). Now, pay
   for all, and end thy prate in Valhall!
  NANNA. Savage, thou mean'st not sure——

HOTHER.   Beware thee, Nanna!

NANNA. Oh, hear me——

HOTHER.   I have seen. Go, hide thee, false one !

NANNA. Thou wilt not sure——

HOTHER.   I will! And now, by Hothbrod,
He dieth by my hand !

BALDER.   Presumptuous mortal !

HOTHER. Thy shield! thy spear! I hate all vaunt, my
   half-god.

NANNA (*rushes towards* BALDER, *who taketh his weapons*).
   O Balder ! noble Balder !

BALDER.   Ah, poor Nanna !
Thou see'st he forces me—that death he beggeth !

HOTHER. Ha! this is all too much. Protect him—hide
   him !
Cover thy gallant with thy faithless bosom !
I will not slay thee ; but my oath is uttered,
That he or I shall fall ! And now !
               [*He turns the point of his spear against himself.*

NANNA.   Ah, Hother !
What doest thou ?

HOTHER.   I've sworn !

NANNA.   Hold, hold, thou savage !
I go—I fly. Oh help, ye gods of heaven !
         [*She goes away in a kind of distraction, but she
            remains standing at the entrance of the scene,
            where she with fearful curiosity looks on and off*

the combatants.   The warriors go in circle with uplifted spears.

HOTHER. Now, valiant Balder, call upon thy father !

BALDER. Shame on thee, Hother !   Thou offendest Nanna.

HOTHER. Prat'st still, my hero ?

BALDER.   Well—thou wilt?

HOTHER.   Ha, Hothbrod !

> [*He casts the spear which he had received from the first* VALKYRIER, *and had retained in his hand. It striketh* BALDER, *but falls, without taking any effect, at his feet.* BALDER *in return casts his spear into his left hand, and tears down a huge piece of the neighbouring rock.*

NANNA. Ye gods of Gevar !

BALDER.   Nanna !

> [*He casts his spear behind him out of the scene.*

NANNA.   Noble being !

HOTHER. Ha ! darest thou mock me, thou inflated brag-gart ?

> [*He takes from the tree the spear which the* Valkyrier, ROTA, *gave him, and casts it.   It strikes so hard against* BALDER'S *breast, that he nearly sinks upon his knee; but it nevertheless falls to the ground without wounding him.*

BALDER. Ha ! Surtur, ha !   Was that the fell destroyer ? Fly from my fury !

HOTHER. Cool its heat in Valhall!

[*He casts the last spear, which he has seized in the meantime, but, like the first, without any apparent effect.*

BALDER (*as he draws his sword*). Now, then, presumptuous?

HOTHER (*as he likewise draws*). Demon! and no half-god!
Thou blunt'st the spear; but here's a sword remaining!
Now, Hothbrod!

[*He strikes at him with his utmost force, but the sword reboundeth from the helm of* BALDER.

BALDER. Odin!

[*He strikes* HOTHER'S *sword from his hand, so that it flies into pieces, seizes him by the arm, and sets his sword against his breast.* HOTHER *sinks upon his knee beneath the powerful grasp, but raises himself immediately, without* BALDER'S *attempting to hinder him but he retains him so in his power that he cannot move himself.* NANNA *rushes in and casts herself down upon her knee before* BALDER.

NANNA. Generous, noble Balder!
BALDER. Take up thy bride and live!
HOTHER. My life detest I,
I would not give the smallest hair of Nanna,
For yet a thousand years thy whole godship!

BALDER. Die, then!

> [*He lifts his sword like one who will strike.*

HOTHER. Why dost delay?

NANNA. Ha! here thou savage!
Here, strike into this breast and spare my bridegroom.

> [BALDER *lets his sword sink.*

HOTHER. Still, still, thou lovest me? Oh, Nanna!
Nanna!

There see'st thou, fiend, she loveth me!

BALDER. Ah, torment!
Ha! I can end thee! [*He lifts his sword again.*

NANNA. Let my tears prevent thee!

HOTHER. By heavens! she's mocking thee! If thou
delayest,

She'll laugh full at thee in the arms of Hother.

NANNA. Believe him not, but virtue — thine own
bosom!

BALDER (*sheathing his sword*). Live, Hother! live!

HOTHER. Ha! have I begged for mercy?

BALDER. No! Live; forget our strife, thou dauntless
warrior!

Embrace thy friend, and be, as erst, unshackled!

HOTHER. Ha! cruel, proud, and all too noble en'my!
Thou know'st, thou feelest but too well thy triumph!
Ha! thou hast overcome, hast humbled Hother!
And think'st thou he can live? Heard, heard has heaven
My oath, that I or Balder die!

[*He grasps his dagger, and is about to stab himself with it, but* BALDER *wrests it out of his hand.*

BALDER. Bethink thee!

HOTHER. Ye heavens! Hother! ah! how art thou fallen!

NANNA (*affectionately*). My Hother!

HOTHER. Ah! farewell for ever, Nanna!

[*He goes hastily away.* NANNA *attempts to follow him, but* BALDER *detains her.*

NANNA, BALDER.

NANNA. Woe's me! he will destroy himself.

BALDER. By Odin!
He shall not! Be composed! believe, I've power
To hinder it! Believe thy Balder, Nanna!

NANNA (*she takes with fervour his hand and bends herself for some time over it*). I do believe thee, noble one, I know thee!
I feel all thy exaltedness. Thy virtues
I hold in reverence. Oh! that all my friendship,
That these hot tears were able to reward thee!

BALDER (*casts himself upon his knees before her*). Oh glimpse! Oh wave of hope, in which I'm drowning!

NANNA (*agitated*). What hopest thou?

BALDER. Let not thy lips, oh Nanna
Awaken Balder from his dream of rapture;

Let him enjoy it; let him read his destiny,
His hope, his life, in yonder precious tear-drops.

NANNA. Ah, what avails it 'gainst one's fate to struggle?
My heart can ne'er of Balder be deserving.

BALDER. Ah, that I but——

NANNA. Excuse me now; thou knowest
I've—— Ah! a miserable friend to comfort.

> [*She tears herself away from him, gives a friendly look
> and goes. He follows her for some time with
> his eyes.*

BALDER. Yet will I hope! Hear, hear ye rocks! that
Balder
Ventures to hope!—stern fate is now contented!
Blunted is Surtur's spear, and Nanna wavers!
Oh virtue! which, when blood rag'd high didst triumph,
How sure, how nobly thou reward'st thy lover!
Ye rocks which so lately gave ear to my groans,
Now hear of my hope and my gladness the tones,
And reply ye proud woods that no longer seem drear;
In vain fate and heaven, oh Balder, have cas'd,
With vigour the bosom thou lovest, and placed
In the hand of the hero the sorcerer's spear.
Oh virtue! thou still dost thy servant befriend;
Ye echoes the triumph of true love extend,
And virtue's fair guerdon proclaim far and near.

THOR, BALDER.

THOR. Boldly resounds thy song, thou friend of battle!

So bluster from the hero's lips the bloody
Hard-gotten vict'ries, and the slain foes' praises,
Whilst he surveys the lonely field of slaughter,
Thou smilest, pleasure from thine eye is flashing,
Like Odin's, when he freed the earth from danger
By watering it with blood of savage giants.

BALDER. Ha, friend! press thou thy breast unto this
    bosom,
And feel what lip but feebly can interpret,
Feel heaven's rapture in my soul!

THOR.   Thou ravest!

BALDER. Ah! Nanna, friend!——

THOR.   Ha'! now I understand thee.
And well it is, full well, that Odin's Balder
At length by tears has soften'd Gevar's daughter!
This triumph——

BALDER.   Thou art mocking!

THOR.   No, thy vict'ry
Shall to me be as one of my most prais'd ones,
As that I won from Nagaard's gloomy demon!
Ha! it is great! It takes from me and Odin
The dastard fear which has too long tormented
Our bosoms. I no more thine ear shall weary
With vain advice. Enough! the maiden loveth.

BALDER. She loveth—yes, by Hæl! she loveth Hother.

THOR. Ha! Balder, dost thou mock me? Whom? What
    Hother?

BALDER. Hast Thor forgotten then the valiant Leir-
King?

THOR (*in thought*). No!—by my hammer, no!—I saw
him battle

At Rolf, the Daneman's festival; I saw him,

Strong in his arm.

BALDER.   But yet it lost the falchion.

THOR (*yet in thought*). Before his spear the copper hau-
berk yielded

Like softest wax.   Shall he—— But scarce a mortal

Avails thereto—— But then if fate——

BALDER.   Banish, oh banish,

These murky thoughts, oh Thor! and share my pleasure.

THOR. Thy pleasure!   Do I dream?   Loves Nanna,
Hother?

BALDER. Ay, doth she!

THOR.   That rejoices thee? Thou ravest.

BALDER. Ah hear!—my joy thou wilt thyself approve of.

THOR (*after some reflection*). Now, noble one, I understand : embrace me—

Thy vict'ry's worthy thee—and me—and Odin.

On Gevar's rocks I will myself engrave it.

Oh! not a weak, soft-hearted maid, but Balder,

But thee, my friend—the monster in thy bosom,

Thy love, thy foolish love, thou overcamest.

BALDER. Ah, hush thee, cruel one! I feel I'm blushing.

Know, I had never o'er my heart less power.

I burn, and tremble at the thought of seeing
The flame put out by which I am tormented.

THOR. What do I hear ?   Ye heavens ! can an Asa
Lose virtue thus, and all—well, quaff thy pleasure !
And rave and dote !   Thou lov'st and art rejected ?
How pleasurably !   By my arm, I'm thinking
The Valkyrie has touch'd thy skull already,
Thou ravest so—I see thy fate is hastening.

BALDER. My fate's first law is love.

THOR.   Alas, the second
Is death !

BALDER. And where's the battle ? where's the slayer ?

THOR. The slayer ?   Hother.

BALDER.   Weaponless, despairing,
He wanders 'mong the rocks.   We fought.

THOR.   He liveth ?

BALDER. Ah, Nanna wept.

THOR.   Curst tears ! the blood of Asa
For ye must pay !

BALDER.   And friend, had he the power,
Think'st thou that Hother, that the Skiolding basely
Would murder him to whom his life he oweth ?

THOR. Not so would he.   But if he must, what can he
'Gainst destiny, if she the death-spear hands him,
And guides herself his arm ?

BALDER.   Oh, banish, banish
Thy timid care, and hear and share my transport ;

Just now, as Hother's life I spar'd there glitter'd,
Through Nanna's tears the first, first glimpse of pity;
Sweetly she smil'd, and granting me her friendship,
She press'd my hand with loving warmth.

    THOR.   Ha! vex not
Mine ear, I pray thee, with thy follies—little
Is Asa Thor with dastard love acquainted;
Yet can I see into her heart. She thanks thee
For Hother's life: that gives thee joy? Thou dreamest.

    BALDER. My life's the dream thou dost aspire to scatter.

    THOR. It is thy death!

    BALDER.   What death? See fate accomplished!
Behold this spear which late the Leir-King brandish'd!
My knee grew weak: I stagger'd when it struck me;
Yet still I live, and it to earth fell blunted.

    THOR (*Whilst he surveys the spear*). Do not deceive thy-
         self, this spear was harden'd
In flames celestial, not in Nastroud's blazes.
But death has greeted Odin's son, and Rota,
She who invites the hero-kings to Valhall,
Is here, where never din of arms resounded.
With terror view'd I battle's haughty daughter:
Dark stood she on a rock, enveiled in vapour;
And on her shoulder, on her steel-cas'd shoulder,
The bird of death, the mournful owl, sat croaking.
Whom seeks she, far from every bloody Champain?
And Surtur's branch, how soon is that discover'd,
If fate but wish! And think'st thou Loke slumbers?

Ah, Balder fly! forget a foolish passion!
Fly, 'ere thy fate, which hasteneth, is accomplish'd.
Follow me straight!

BALDER.   What—fly! and give up Nanna!
The hope in which I live is far too noble
For me to fly from it.

THOR.   O Balder, hear me!
Hear why I come, and if thou wish'st for rescue,
Then heed a friend's, a father's last, last warning!
Wondering at thy infatuation, troubled
By threatening, now no longer dark forebodings,
By panic seiz'd, press'd by unwonted sadness,
I left these hills, and thunder-peals announced me
In Asgaard, every eye my trouble notic'd;
Straightway around me stream'd the eldest Aser,
Each first would know, what grief, or rather terror,
Press'd down my eye.   But straight Allfather made me
A sign: he blushes, Balder, at thy weakness!
He bade me keep it, whilst we could, a secret,
And question first once more the ancient Mimer.
I question'd him, and murky fate's explorer
Thus answer'd: " If the sun (ah, hear and tremble,
And save thee, whilst thou canst!) if it to-morrow,
When by its glories yonder hills are brighten'd,
Which oft have echoed back the half-god's wailings,
Behold him yet in love and yet rejected,
Then likewise it beholds the spear which slays him,
And Odin's tears and all the Aser's sorrow! "

BALDER. Time presses, then.   Excuse me, Thor ; I hasten
With tears to soften Nanna's noble bosom,
To move her with my prayer, and, lowly kneeling,
My doom demand, be't life or death ; for quickly
Shall Balder's fate disclose itself.   [*He goes.*

    THOR (*whilst he looks after him with compassion*). Ah,
      madman !
Headlong thou hurriest to meet destruction !

ACT THE THIRD.

It is dark night.   The storm howls among the rocks.   Some-
    times it lightens and thunders, and the bears bellow here
    and there in the forest.

    HOTHER (*sitting upon a rock unarmed and in a dejected*
      attitude).

        The rocks are reeling,
        When storms are roaring,
        And thunders pealing,
         I feel no fright !
        What I'm enduring
        Is wilder, stranger
        Than thunder's anger
         Or tempests might.
Welcome, thou night ! O darkness thick ! how friendly,
Compassionately hid'st thou me from Hother !
From him, the weak, the overcome, the fallen !

Come, then, embrace me, Hœtheim's murky princess!
With all thy horrors dark, thou foe of gladness!
Ah, come! conceal the feeble, shiver'd weapon!
Cover the gloomy rock where I—— Ha! thunder
Annihilate thee, accursed thought, that darest
Disturb the Skoldung where to rest he's flung him!
But I may breathe it to the night, and Hœtheim
I may entrust with Hother's ignominy.
Ha! hear it, night! and in thy depths conceal it!
There is a rock—a gloomy one—a horrid,
For ugly demons swarm upon its summit,
And dragons nestle in its murky caverns:
There did I fall, and with me fell my honour.
There knelt I powerless, and my life accepted!
Now am I calm, for I no more behold it;
Nor yet behold the proud, the noble foeman,
Nor yet my Nanna's cheek, o'erspread with blushes;
Nor yet the burning, hated tears which rescued,
Which purchased Hother from triumphant Balder!
Ha! storm, thou sinkest! Howl and whoop around me!
Peal, thunders, peal! and drown the cruel echo
Of dastard prayer, of Nanna's intercession!

> Life of my Nanna,
> Thy breath doth kill,
> Its sweet lamenting,
> One stroke preventing,
> With many, with many
> This breast doth fill.

Thou lovest me! Ha! weak, enamour'd Nanna!
Thou lovest Hother's life, but not thy Hother.
How cold, how cruel to his name, his honour!
But I—I too was cruel! I accus'd thee——
Beloved Nanna, at thy feet full quickly
Hother's best blood shall wash away that insult!

        [*He springs up and walks about the scene.*

Why do I slumber? Why delay a moment
To keep my oath? Ha, cruel, cruel destiny!
E'en death itself thou dost refuse to Hother,
For every sword and precipice thou hidest;
Ha, feeble spear! whereon I, fool-like, trusted,
Where art thou now? and thou my fragile Mimring
Ne'er frail in fight before; and thou my dagger——

        [*He stumbles over the horn which he cast away in the
          first act.*

What, what is this? By Hal, the horn which Vanfred
Gave me wherewith in time of need to call him.
Ha! by the gods, was ever need so horrid,
To crave to die, yet want the power of dying;
Friendship so warm as his will never surely
Refuse a dagger to this breast.

        [*He winds the horn, which echoes frightfully among
          the rocks.*

                Ha, Vanfred!
I call thee now; where art thou, Vanfred? Vanfred!

        [*A whirlwind is heard, and* LOKE *immediately
          appears.*

LOKE, HOTHER.

LOKE. Hail, hail to thee, most fortunate of heroes!

HOTHER. Ha! darest thou mock Hother?

LOKE.   What disturbeth
A fortune which thy foe himself, which Skulda,
Which heavenly and subterranean powers
Establish with united strength?

HOTHER.   Old dreamer!
Lend me a spear, and better right hand shall
Establish it than all the powers thou namest!

LOKE. I know thy state of mind and wretched project.
By Nastroud, that worst of fools, if Balder
Had not thine eyes with Asa magic blinded,
And hid each dagger, each abyss thou soughtest,
Ere now in mist thou'dst unreveng'd been lying!

HOTHER. What, has he hindered me, the noble, proud one!

LOKE. Yes, proud; for he despises thee.

HOTHER.   Despises!

LOKE. And think'st thou he for sake of pleasing Nanna
Would e'er have deign'd to guard thee from destruction,
If he had much regarded Hother's anger,
And if thy love one grain of sand he heeded?

HOTHER. Bad art thou, Vanfred; all thy words are
    poison'd.

LOKE (*incensed*). Ha! Hother, thou reward'st in evil
    fashion
The friendship and the happiness I bring thee.

E

HOTHER. What happiness ?

LOKE.   But come, thy misery sours thee;
Know, I can straight assuage it !

HOTHER.   And delayest.

LOKE. Know then at once, thou lucky son of Hothbrod,
The spear which sendeth Balder's soul to Hælheim.

HOTHER. A spear, a spear ! 'tis all I——

LOKE.   Is discover'd !
I knew, for I had read it in the planets,
Valhalla's battle-loving maids must seek for
The ne'er seen weapon, and prepare for slaughter
Its deadly point, and I—yes, I—seduc'd them,
The haughty three, to seek the spear.

HOTHER.   Seduc'd them ?

LOKE. And dost thou think they wish the death of Balder?

HOTHER. Ha, Vanfred ! more.

LOKE.   At first thou hadst not the right one ;
Thy combat, friend, prov'd that.   Near then had
Balder crush'd thee and my design.   Aghast I saw him
Brandish the Jotun's bane—I'm well acquainted
With Balder's strength ; but ha ! the fool prov'd tender ;
He saw thy bride, and spar'd thee.   Then up mounted
My courage and thine own.

HOTHER (*to himself*).   I blush : my courage !
(*To Loke*). What, courage ! I was raging—blind with fury !

LOKE. Courage of fury—I, by Hæl, care little,
My youthful hero, which thine eyeball gleams with,

If thou seek vengence, and thine enemy falleth.

    HOTHER. Who art thou—who? But speak; proceed;
        explain thee!

    LOKE. Strong was thine arm, and strong 'gainst Jotun's
        armour

Was Rota's lance, but all too weak 'gainst Balder;

And yet he kneel'd; I saw the proud one palen.

But ha! he rear'd himself; my heart then fail'd me,

For I could best appreciate thy full danger;

Raised was his arm; bright appear'd the massive falchion;

He called on Odin's name, and then none living

Could save thee but himself—the fool! his lofty

Courage shall prove his overthrow.

    LOTHER.   Ha, Vanfred!

    LOKE. Well?

    HOTHER.   I do admire more and more thy wisdom.

But whilst we fought, where were the maids of battle.

    LOKE. They were my dread; I quak'd at every shadow

And every leaf that mov'd, lest I should see them.

When I saw that no one of the sisters

Heard the high call, and din of shield and falchion,

My courage rose—I knew thou wast in safety:

They hear no fight where no one's doomed to perish.

    HOTHER. And now the spear thou spak'st about?

    LOKE.   She has it,

Valfather's favour'd maid—his trusty servant,

At length discover'd by unwearied searching

The spear by which his much-lov'd son shall perish.
Shortly ere thou didst call, as in my cavern
I sat, its vaulted roof begun to tremble.
Three times my stilly dwelling shook, and o'er me
A sound assailed my ear; 'twas like the tempest's
When it uptears the mountain oak; then heard I
The voice of Rota; black huge drops did trickle
Of Jotun blood, of them whom Odin slaughtered,
Through the rock's rifts.   I knew by all these signals
That she had found the right, the fatal weapon.

HOTHER (*impatiently*). Where is it—where?

LOKE.   She hardens it in Nastroud.

HOTHER. Peace, dreamer!   Go!

LOKE.   I see this heat with pleasure,
And to extinguish all thy doubts, I'll show thee—
If thou dare see her—the terrific Rota.

HOTHER. What, Vanfred! if I dare?

LOKE.   Enough!   Look westward!

[*He touches* HOTHER'S *eyelids.   Immediately is seen
      the entrance of a vast cavern, which is only
      illumined by the flames which, with a continual
      roaring, now sinking, now rising, appear in its
      deepest part.   At the entrance, on each side, is a
      little round altar.   On the one a flame is burn-
      ing in which lies the fatal spear.   On the other
      stands a caldron.   The* VALKYRIER *move in a
      circle round the first.*

THE THREE VALKYRIER.

The first. Flames of Nastroud
          Blaze away !
     The deepmost deeps feel
          Valhall's May.

The second. Flames whose roaring
          With dismay
     E'en Asa hears,
          Fate's voice obey.

ROTA. Poisonous blazes
     Harden a spear
     For Valhall's May !

All three. Poisonous blazes
     Harden a spear
     For Valhall's May.

ROTA. Whom it woundeth
          It shall slay.

The first. Whom it woundeth
          It shall slay.

The second. Whom it woundeth
          It shall slay.

All three. Whom it woundeth
          It shall slay.

ROTA (*takes the spear from the fire and goes towards the other altar*). Enough, enough! Now will we in the caldron

Cool its red point—now backward turns the circle,

And as we turn, the life of him turns backward

Whom the spear smites; as quench'd are Nastroud's
   sparkles

Vanish shall the life of him it woundeth.

> [*She retains the spear in her hand, and all three*
> *march round the caldron.*

All three.   In juice of rue,
                  And trefoil too;
                  In marrow of bear
                     And blood of Trold,
                  Be cool'd the spear,
                     Three times cool'd,
                  When not from blazes
                  Which Nastroud raises
                     For Valhall's May.

ROTA (*she dips it in, and then immediately gives it to the*
   first VALKYRIE, *who does the same, and then hands it*
   to the second,   likewise dips it in the caldron;
   meanwhile they sing :)

The first.   Whom it woundeth
                  It shall slay.

The second.   Whom it woundeth
                  It shall slay.

All three.   Whom it woundeth
                  It shall slay

[ROTA *takes the spear. The* VALKYRIER *and the cavern disappear. The scene appears the same as in the first of this act. The tempest still continues to rage.*

HOTHER. Evanished! sunken! sorcery surroundeth
My every step, and ties the arm of Hother.
Fool that I am ! the moon will soon break over
Gevar's high rocks; and I, by Hothbrod's ashes,
Like one who fearfully will prolong existence,
I'm paying heed to phantoms. Vanfred ! Vanfred !
Fiend, who didst vow me friendship I detested !
Say, where is now the spear which kills for certain ?

LOKE. Thou saw'st it.

HOTHER.   Ha ! I saw ! I saw ! Where is it ?

LOKE. Do I not know that Odin's maids prepar'd it
Only for thee, that fate will only suffer
Thine arm in Balder's heart to thrust it ?

HOTHER.   Lately
Thou saidst, think'st thou they wish the death of Balder ?
But now against him they the weapon harden ;
Now Valhall's maidens hate the noble half-god.
Hence with thy contradictions, false deceiver !

LOKE. I have already said that I seduced them ;
My subtlety, not they, the spear has harden'd.

HOTHER. Good now ! thy subtlety ! how nobly Hother
Passes the night ! Proceed with thy narration.

LOKE. Then hear. Thou dost remember Rota's present.

The spear which set the haughty half-god kneeling,
That shiver'd I, and brought it unto Rota.
I borrowed Tyr's, the Asa's dress and figure.
" Behold," I cried, " thy spear, thou crafty Rota !
Late at a Jotun's foot I found it lying,
Sent from the Leir-King's hand ; it still was buzzing,
For strong is Hother's arm ; I knew the weapon,
And I, who trusted in thy art, I shouted.
Now ill it stands with yonder mountain Jotun ;
But loud he laugh'd, and straight the lance upsnatching,
He shiver'd it, and here, O crafty Rota !
Here bring I back to thee the precious fragments ! "
With joy I saw her eyes with fury flashing,
She swore by Odin's arm, by all the powers,
And by the highest Godhead—by Allfather,
Restless to search till she a spear discover'd
With power to slay the strongest son of Ymer,
And all who could be slain.   She swore and vanished.
Then seem'd it—then, by Hæla's mists, then seem'd it
As if fate only for that oath had waited.
Three times above me thunder'd the high Norna ;
She spake ; but terrible is Skulda's thunder ;
I cannot bear its sound ; I swift departed ;
But soon was conscious of our spear's discovery.
Then thou didst call——   But hear the heavy pinions !
'Tis she ! 'tis Rota ! I aside must hasten ;
For Valhall's maids detest me.   [LOKE *goes aside.*

HOTHER, *and presently the* Valkyrie ROTA.

HOTHER (*he pursues* LOKE *with a contemptuous look*).
                                                    Outcast!
Ha! dastard slave! and thou didst swear me friendship!
No, ne'er hast thou been Hother's friend, thou traitor,
But the sworn enemy of the gods and virtue!

 ROTA (*handing him the fatal spear with a half-averted
  countenance*). Here, son of Hothbrod! here, my much-
 lov'd warrior!
Receive this spear, and use it as——

 HOTHER.   Thou weepest!

 ROTA. Thou saw'st my tear—dear and noble the blood is
Which it forebodes; but do thou use this weapon!
Yet 'tis no gift of mine—'tis that of Skulda.

 HOTHER. I know thou fearest for the generous Balder;
But, noble maid, if thou my heart see'st into,
Thou know'st that he is safe as Thor in Valhall.

 ROTA. Think'st thou to thwart the Norna's will, young
  hero?
She pointed out the hidden tree; she bade me
Break off the bough of death; she bade me harden
Its point in Nastroud's flames; she—— But what will I?
My tears are wasted, like thy noble project.
Well, then: use thou this spear! Death is its surname,
And whom it smites eternal sleep shall fetter
In Hælheim's silent night, if he is mortal;

The immortal demon, whose eye by hate and wickedness
Is clouded, 'twill plunge to torments of a thousand
    winters.
Mark that, and use it well! Thy breast is noble;
But him, the wretch! who breathest poison in it,
(Full well I know he's near) him shalt thou punish.

                           [ROTA *disappears.*

         HOTHER, *and presently* LOKE.

   HOTHER. Now, now! is all a dream? Yet, I've the
    weapon!
Now welcome death! my noble foe no longer
Shall hide thee from me, nor of thee deprive me;
Now can I keep what I have sworn! O Nanna!
I bring a noble offering to thy virtue!

      [*He is going, but* LOKE *meets him at the entrance.*
  LOKE. Whither? thou Fortune's fav'rite!
  HOTHER (*sharply*).   Ha! to Hælheim.
  LOKE. Hother, I scoff thy wise determination.
  HOTHER (*incensed*). Thou scoffest?
  LOKE.   Yes, thou holdest thy foeman's life,
And thou wilt die.
  HOTHER.   What foeman's?
  LOKE. Whose, if not Balder's?
  HOTHER.   Ah, my life he gave me!
And though I hold the gift in little value,
I took it still. And shall his lofty spirit

His downfall prove?   Shall I, shall Hother punish
The pity I craved not?

LOKE.   By Hæl! he's coming!
Waste not the moments in these foolish visions.

HOTHER. What wouldst thou?

LOKE.   Stand behind that pine, and kill him!

HOTHER. Ha! dastard slave!

> [*He strikes* LOKE *on the head with the spear, and he
> instantly sinks howling into the earth.   He is
> no sooner out of sight than everything becomes
> quiet.   The sun rises in its full majesty.   After*
> HOTHER *has for some time looked on all this with
> astonishment, he says* :

>   Like thee fall every traitor
Who breatheth wickedness in the Skiolding's bosom!
Ha, Balder!   [*He goes somewhat aside.*

HOTHER, BALDER.

BALDER (*without perceiving* HOTHER).   Gloomy was this
    night and horrid!
Around about me angry gods consulted.
What seek they?   To affright the soul of Balder?
Now all is still.

HOTHER.   Now unconcern'd and haughty
Walks the high demigod!   Ah, little thinks he
Each breath he draweth is the gift of Hother.

BALDER. Who utter'd Hother's name? I heard it utter'd,
But all is hushed as death.   I know not wherefore
That name affects me more than any other,
And why within mine ear 'tis ever buzzing.
Ah! can I more than pity him, poor mortal!
Who now his life and feebleness bewaileth,
And trembles weaponless at his own shadow.

    HOTHER. Ha, now! for that is worthy of the Skoldung;
I'll be as proud as thou, and fly thy presence!   [*He goes.*

    BALDER. Who's speaking here?   Who dares disturb my
       musings?
But, know I not that Finnish fiends are swarming
Upon the rocks?   The sun approach'd the ocean,
And yet I found not Nanna : all deserted
Was Gevar's house, and hollow rang each echo
Of Balder's sighs.   Where was she, then? where was she?
Ah! Hother charm'd thee.   In the arms of Hother
Thou didst not hear my sighs, my timid knocking,
And my enamour'd call, thou cruel maiden!
And what if I had found thee?   Then thine answer
Most probably had prov'd the death of Balder.
I know myself no more; my heart it flutters,
And here about it creeps unwonted chillness.
Yes, Nanna! yes; 'twas thou taught'st me to tremble.
Ah! belov'd maiden!   I, a half-god, tremble
When thou but breathest, when thy lip thou movest,
As if to utter No, thy lip is open'd.

Oh, hush ! and let me sink with hope to Hælheim !
But did I not behold thine eye beam friendship
On Balder ? felt I not thy warm tear trickle
Upon this hand ? and saw I not thy blushes ?
Ha ! I'll think through, I will enjoy entirely
My hope : why then, my heart, beat'st thou so wildly ?
And why in Balder's eyes are tears uprising,
And hope to me a stranger ?   Oh, my treasure,
Thou teachest me a dastard's fear !   I tremble
Now I've a glimpse of hope to be depriv'd of.
Ah ! if 'tis torn from me again, if Nanna——
Oh doubt ! oh fear with which my heart is tortur'd !
Yes, Thor, my friend, thy words were truth and
        wisdom ;
That pity that she showed was thanks for sparing Hother :
She trembled but for Hother—for the lov'd one :
Each tear but begged his life.   What cruel delusion
Has led my soul astray ?   Ah, wretched meteor
Of empty hope ! thou, thou for me couldst glitter,
As if I had been ignorant of her hatred.
Ha ! she has ever fled my path, my shadow ;
And when, to my own torment, once I wrested
From the proud maid some sort of heed and answer,
'Twas mockery mere : she called herself unworthy
To be great Balder's bride and Odin's daughter,
And held my love-sick sighs for jest and flatt'ry.
Yet never have I heard the word which killeth,

Without the aid of Surtur's deadly sapling—
The No, the frightful No, by Nanna utter'd.
Ha! I will hear it!   Yes, by Hælheim's darkness!
My tears shall now' extract that No from Nanna.

NANNA, BALDER.

NANNA (*she rushes distractedly in upon the stage*). Ah!
      No one answers me!   Do thou give hearing
To Nanna's hard rock, which no god heedeth!
My anguish ease!   Reply!   Ah, where's my lov'd one?
    BALDER (*aside*). My fate will have it so.   Ha, Nanna.
    NANNA.   Show me,
Ye silent forests, shades once lov'd, now awful,
Oh, show me him—disclose me my dearest!
    BALDER (*aside*). Ha! shall I?   Dare I?
    NANNA.   Ah, where art thou, Hother?
Perhaps in an abyss, all crushed and bloody
And silent!   Woe is me! for ever silent!
    BALDER (*springing to her*). Dear Nanna!   Oh what
        terror——
    NANNA.   Ha! I've seen him!
The direst dream has shown to me my Hother!
Close by a yawning chasm was he standing,
And round about him bellow'd hideous monsters.
    BALDER. Thine—as thou callest him—thine Hother
      liveth.

NANNA (*whilst she recognizes* BALDER). Ha Balder! thou
    hast slain him! Ah, forgive me!
My dream confuses me—thou see'st I tremble.
I heard the fall of gods—the gods lamenting ;
And bloody by the Hall there stood a spectre :
Big was the ruddy wound whereto it pointed.
Like one deep musing it conceal'd its visage ;
But big the tears were through its fingers streaming :
Ah, the pale son of night was tall as Hother!

    BALDER. Ha! Hother can't be dead.

    NANNA.   I do believe thee ;
But ah! I cannot rest—I cannot, Balder,
Till I have seen his face, have spoken to him,
Embrac'd his arm, and press'd it to this bosom.

    BALDER (*distractedly*). Ha, Nanna! this is more—'tis
    more, by Odin,
Than I can bear!

    NANNA (*terrified*). Ye mighty gods of heaven!
Thou fright'nest me, forlorn one!

       [*She endeavours to escape, but* BALDER *detains her by
       force, and flings himself at her feet.*

    BALDER.   Oh my Nanna!
Stay! by these burning tears I do adjure thee,
By all my sufferings! Stay, oh stay!

    NANNA (*with disquiet*).   What wilt thou?

    BALDER. I scarcely know! Ah! I have hop'd, dear
    Nanna!

NANNA. Unhand me ! Let me fly ! What hast thou hop'd
  for ?
Thou know'st who has my love.   Unhand me, Balder !
  BALDER. No, by the gods ! here at thy feet I'll hear thee
Pronounce my doom.   Is there no hope remaining ?
Can all my tenderness—these tears—can nothing
Soften thy cruelty ?   Oh, answer, Nanna !
Say so at once !   Plunge in my heart the dagger !
  NANNA. Ah, wherefore, Balder, dost thou love a mortal ?
  BALDER. Perhaps thou doubtest my love, perhaps thou
  wishest
Its whole extent.   Ha, towards Heaven
I'll lift my better hand, and vow eternal,
Eternal tenderness to thee, my Nanna !
If greater proofs thou wish'st for, do but name them,
That I may show to thee how dear I love the !
  NANNA. Ah, Balder, spare me ! spare thyself !   What
  wilt thou ?
How often have I said my heart can never
Merit the like of thee !
  BALDER.   Accurst evasion !
Why dost thou seek to spare me ?   Crush me ! kill me !
Say that thou never wilt !
  NANNA.   Ah, I love Hother !
How can I ?
  BALDER. Perhaps thou only think'st thou lov'st him.
Can he deserve thee, Nanna ? he, a mortal ?

NANNA (*incensed*). He loveth virtue, Balder; he is
  valiant,
And great is he 'mongst kings; he ruleth over
The Danes !

BALDER. I'm more than any king, oh Nanna !

NANNA. Wert thou a god, I'd still have none but
  Hother !

BALDER (*stretches his right hand despairingly towards
  heaven*). Although rejected—hear it all ye heavens—
Although rejected, I will love thee, Nanna !

> [*He has scarcely finished speaking when the* Valkyrie
> ROTA *appears. The Bird of Death sits upon
> her shoulder. She averts her countenance, touches
> his skull with her spear, and says :*

To battle, friend ! to wounds, and fall, and darkness !

> [*She immediately disappears, and as* BALDER *and*
> NANNA *have their backs turned to her, and have
> both been too attentive to themselves to observe
> any one else, she is neither seen nor heard but by
> the spectators.*

BALDER (*he springs up like a maniac, and holds his hand
  for some time before his head*). Ha ! how I'm dream-
  ing ! how I waste my moments
In dastard sighs, bewailing like a woman !
And have I not a shield and sword ? To battle !
To battle, Balder ! Let thy broad sword glitter !
Lift high the sword, cleave down the haughty warrior,

F

And dip thy spear in blood, thou son of Odin !
Ha ! din of shield 'gainst shield, and battle's bellow,
They, they shall gladden me—and deafen Nanna !
And I will cool this heart in blood of Kempions !

   [*He draws his sword, and runs away in madness.*

 NANNA (*alone*). Ye heavens ! what did he mean ? Alas,
  he rages !

Wretch that I am ! he goes to slay my Hother !

   My hopes ye annih'late,
    Ye powers of the sky !
   Who'll strengthen me, fainting,
    Against the god's might ?
   Who'll heed my lamenting,
    My sorrowful plight ?
   Ah ! whom can I wend to ?
   Will earth e'er attend to
    A powerless cry,
   Which cruel gods smile at ?
   My hopes ye annih'late,
    Ye powers of the sky !

Ha ! ye have crush'd my heart ! Oh Hother ! Hother !
Where art thou ? Ah ! I can no more ! I'm swooning !
O Death ! O Freya !

   [*She supports herself, fainting, against a tree.*

   HOTHER, NANNA.

HOTHER (*he rushes up to her in alarm*). Dearest !

NANNA (*looking stiffly upon him*).   Ah ! my Hother !

HOTHER. So wild ! so pale ! Ah ! would thy noble
  bosom

Was not so tender !

NANNA.   Voice of my belov'd one !

Oh, speak again ! Oh, speak again !

HOTHER.   Thou tremblest,

My bride ! my much-lov'd bride ! And burning tear-
  drops,

Oh, hide them ! Ha ! they burn me—melt my courage !

Weep not, my bride !

NANNA.   Ah, joy ! the joy of heaven,

Entices forth these tears ! My Hother liveth !

HOTHER (*mournfully*). Still liveth !

NANNA (*affectionately and sorrowfully*). Still !

HOTHER (*turning away his face*). O cruel, cruel fortune !

Yet I have sworn ?

NANNA.   Fright me not, my Hother !

Affright me not ! What mean'st thou ? Mighty powers !

Thine eyes thou turnest from thy bride !

HOTHER (*looking upon her with tenderness*). Ah, Nanna !

NANNA. Ha ! tears on Hother's cheeks ! Oh, save me,
  Freya !

What means this ? Oh, I die !

HOTHER (*he embraces her with violence*). Oh, dearest
  Nanna !

F 2

NANNA. Oh heaven ! say——

HOTHER (*embraces her again*). Once more, my bride !

NANNA.   I tremble
What means this ?

HOTHER.   Canst thou bury in oblivion
Thy Hother's cruel doubt ?   Say, canst thou pardon
His only crime ?

NANNA.   Think'st thou I can remember
That Hother e'er has err'd ?

HOTHER.   How nobly spoken !
Farewell, my bride ! farewell, for ever.

>   [*He embraces her for the third time, and is going ; but*
>   *she holds fast his arm.*

NANNA.   Cruel !
If thou hast ever lov'd me——

HOTHER.   Canst thou doubt it ?
By Odin, more than the best light !   Can Hother's
Tears not make bare to thee his heart ?

NANNA   Then wherefore
Wouldst thou fly from me !

HOTHER.   Honour calleth—Honour !
And that—forgive me—that is more than Nanna.
Ha ! I must fly from thee !   Each tear thou sheddest
Enfeebles but my heart, and makes death bitter.

>   [*He is going.*

NANNA. If thou regard'st my vow—regard'st my terror,
Wouldst thou not see me die, and die distracted——

HOTHER. What wilt thou ?

NANNA.   Ah ! a prayer !—oh how I tremble——
But if thou meetest Balder——

HOTHER.   I avoid him !

NANNA (*astonished, and calmer*). What ! thou avoid'st
    him ?

HOTHER.   Think'st thou I bear hatred
'Gainst one who yielded thee a glimpse of pleasure ?
One—nearly one of Hother's days ?   He gave me
My life, and shall I slay him in requital ?
Oh ! Nanna, . . . I've the mighty thought imagined ;
But with it trembles yet my lip—oh, canst thou
Pay virtue its reward—forget for ever thy Hother,
And—in course of time—love Balder ?

NANNA. Oh, hush ! oh, hush ! my Hother !

HOTHER.   He is virtuous,
He loves thee well, and Odin is his father.

NANNA. How cruel !

HOTHER.   I must fly from thee for ever !

NANNA. Oh horror ! Whither ? What is thy intention ?

HOTHER. To die ! Thou know'st my oath ! Ha ! the sun
    hastens !
Seest thou how high ?   I swore by Hothbrod's ashes
With Balder not to live a day ! Release me !
Ha ! seest thou how high——

NANNA.   And I have sworn too,
By tenderness, by Freya, by my bosom,

I'll not release thee; I thy track will follow
In the black night of death! This arm I'll cling to,
And my tear-moisten'd eye, until it bursteth,
Shall gaze on thee, shall gaze on thee, its Hother!

HOTHER. Then be courageous—of thy Hother worthy!
Think on his oath, and——

NANNA (*she releases him*). Ah, what wilt thou, Hother?
HOTHER. And see him die!

> [*He lifts his spear to stab himself. At that same moment the frantic* BALDER *rushes upon the scene.*

BALDER, HOTHER, NANNA.

BALDER (*he runs directly up to* NANNA). Come! follow
    me now, Nanna!
Our bridal festival's prepar'd in Hælheim,
In Asgaard. Follow me, thou murky daughter
Of joy! Ha, quick! Of dastard love I dream not.
Jotuns await my arm. Hurrah! thou stayest!
Thou stayest! Come!

> [*He seizes her by the arm, and seeks to drag her away by force.* HOTHER *steps between, and endeavours to thrust him aside with his hand.*

NANNA.   Oh, save me! save me, Hother!
HOTHER. Hold, Balder!

BALDER (*he releases* NANNA, *and drawing his sword, hews
at* HOTHER *with his utmost might, who seeks to parry
the blow with his spear, retreating at the same time*).
Fall, presumptuous wretch !

HOTHER.   Beware thee !

BALDER. Fall, nidding !

HOTHER.   Ha, beware thee !

BALDER.   Die !

[*He stumbles, and runs the spear into his breast;
whereupon he immediately drops his sword and
sinks upon one knee.*

HOTHER.   Ha, Balder !

BALDER. Ha, Nanna !—Thor ! I have deserv'd my
fortune.

[*He dies, and a mighty whirlwind passes over the
scene.*

NANNA. Ye heavens !

HOTHER.   He is dead, the mighty Balder !

A voice far away in the forest. He is dead, the mighty
Balder !

Many voices, which answer one another amongst the rocks.
The mighty Balder is dead.

[*It thunders;* ODIN *and* FRIGGA *appear upon a cloud
in a very mournful attitude.* THOR *and many
of the* ASER *come forward from one side of the
wood, and the three* VALKYRIER *from the other.*

THOR (*and his retinue*). Odin, thy Balder is dead !

Chorus.   Thunders, burst your cloudy portals!
             Heaven, earth, and ocean rave!
             Weep ye gods, and mourn ye mortals,
             O'er the mighty Balder's grave!

THOR.   Gods of battle stern and gory,
             Weep ye o'er the hero slain!
             Balder, thou the Aser's glory!
             Love, base love, has prov'd thy bane

Chorus.   Balder, thou the Aser's glory,
             Love, base love, has prov'd thy bane.

ROTA.   I of slaughter swift purveyor,
             Sorrow o'er the hero slain!
             Balder, thou the Jotun-slayer,
             Loke's falsehood was thy bane.

Chorus.   Balder, thou the Jotun-slayer,
             Loke's falsehood was thy bane.

HOTHER. Hother's burning tears are flowing
             O'er the mighty Balder slain;
             Ah, thy heart with virtue glowing,
             Noble Balder, was thy bane.

Chorus.   Ah, thy heart with virtue glowing,
             Noble Balder, was thy bane.

NANNA.   Nanna weeps with pallid feature
             O'er the mighty Balder slain:
             Friend of gods and every creature!
             Fate alone has prov'd thy bane.

Chorus.   Friend of gods and every creature !
        Fate alone has prov'd thy bane.

Many voices answer one another among the rocks. The
    mighty Balder is dead !

Concluding chorus. Thunders, burst your cloudy portals !
        Heaven, earth, and ocean rave !
        Weep and howl, ye gods and mortals,
        O'er the mighty Balder's grave.

EXPLANATION OF THE MYTHOLOGICAL WORDS AND NAMES.

ALLFATHER was one of Odin's surnames, but it signifies in this piece the highest being, who governs all things, and Odin himself.

ALF, a spirit; the same as Demon amongst the Greeks. There were good and bad Alfs or Elves, light and black, as the Edda calls them.

ASER. As was one of Odin's surnames, and on that account the name of Aser was given to all the gods.

ASGARD, the castle or city of the gods, erected by Odin and his brothers.

THE FALL OF ASGARD. At the end of the world the heavens were to burst, and the castle of the gods to fall.

BALDER, son of Odin and Frigga, the best and most beautiful amongst the Aser. His death and the circumstances which caused it in this piece—that is, the whole plot—are taken partly from the Edda (43rd, 44th and 45th falle), partly from the third book of Saxo, and something is, according to poetic license, added or altered.

FENRI's WOLF, was begot by Loke with the giantess Angerbode. This wolf in the conflict of Surtur with the gods was to swallow Odin, who on account of this prophecy kept him in chains.

FIGHT AND DEATH OF GODS. At the destruction of the world, Odin and the other gods were to fight with Surtur and his train, and all to perish in this conflict. This period is termed, in the Edda, Ragnarokr, the "twilight of the gods."

FIND, a Trold or Demon of this name.

FREYA, the most exalted of the goddesses next to Frigga. She was the protectress of the human race in general, but particularly of lovers.

FRIGGA, the wife of Odin and the mother of Balder ; the most exalted of all the goddesses.

GELDER, king of the Saxons (according to Saxo, in the life of Hother). He is presumed here to have been killed by Hother, who is therefore called " the bane of Gelder."

GEVAR, according to Saxo, a spæman or prophet, the father of Nanna and the foster-father of Hother. He makes him likewise king of Norway ; but Giver is not so in this piece.

HÆL or HÆLA, the goddess of death. She was the daughter of Loke and the giantess Angerbode, and was hurled down by Odin to her horrible habitation.

HÆLHEIM, Hæl's dwelling. In the Edda it is called Helim, that is, Hell ; but as the word Hell has now a different signification, it was necessary to invent here a word to express Hæl's dwelling.

HÆLWAY, the way of the dead, or the path to Hælbeim.

HERTE, HERTA, or HERTHA, the earth, considered as a divine being and worshipped as a goddess by the old German and Northern people, as likewise by the Romans and others. The Edda calls this goddess Jürd (that is, earth), and makes her the daughter and wife of Odin, and the mother of Thor, his first son.

HERTEDAL, the place in Sielland where Herte's grove was.

HOTHBROD, the father of Hother, according to Saxo, who makes him king of Sweden, and thus Hother a Swede. Contrary to which, the author of this piece found himself justified in reckoning Hother amongst the Skioldungs.

HOTHER, according to Saxo, was king of Denmark and Sweden ; but his Life, by the same, is a chain of fables, which has yet given considerable occasion to the contents of this piece.

LEIRE, the ancient place of residence of the Danish kings, whence they were termed " Kings of Leire."

LIDSKIALF, in the Edda Klidskialf, a place in Asgard from which Odin surveys the whole world.

LOKE, a very wicked god, who, according to the Edda, was the cause of the death of Balder, and was therefore conducted by the other gods to a cavern, where they chained him to three rocks, there to suffer the most painful punishment until the destruction of the world. By the giantess Angerbode he begot Fenri's Wolf, Midgard's Serpent, and Hæl. He was reckoned among the Aser, and was, notwithstanding his wickedness, beautiful of appearance.

MIDGARD'S SERPENT, a serpent begot by Loke with the giantess Angerbode. It was to be one of the occasioners of the world's destruction, and was on that account cast by Odin into the deep sea, where it grew to such a degree that it lay round the whole earth, and bit its own tail.

MIMMER, the owner of a fountain wherein wisdom and knowledge of the future lay concealed, out of which he drank every morning. Odin was once obliged to lay one of his eyes in pawn, in order to obtain a draught from this fountain. He was likewise, when Surtur should attack the gods, to ride to this fountain and seek counsel from Mimer on his own and his army's account.

MIMRING, this is the sword called here, which Hother, according to the relation of Saxo, took from a satyr or wild man of the same name.

NANNA, daughter of Gevar, beloved by Hother, and by Balder, son of Odin, according to Saxo, whose narration bears that Hother wedded Nanna, and afterwards slew Balder by the assistance of an enchanted belt which three nymphs had bestowed upon him.

NASTROUD, was properly the place where the ungodly were to be after the destruction of the world, but here the word is intended to signify the glowing and burning world towards the south, at whose extremest end Surtur had his habitation, and which is called in the Edda, Muspel, or Muspelheim.

NORNIES, were the goddesses of destiny, whose messages Odin himself was compelled to fear and to attend to. They were three in number. But the eldest, Urd (been), presided over the past; the second, Verande (being), the present; and the youngest, Skuld (shall be), the future.

ODIN, the god of war, the most exalted of the gods, and father of them all.

ROTA, one of the Valkyrier. See VALKYRIER.

SKIOLDUNG. Skiold, son of Odin, was the founder of the Danish monarchy. His descendants were called after him Skioldungs, or, contractedly, Skiolds.

Skulda (*in the Edda*, Skuld), the youngest Nornie. See Nornies.

Surtur (*the Black*), the ruler of the glowing or burning world, at whose extremest end was his seat or dwelling. See above : Nastroud. At the fated time he was with his army to overcome and slaughter Odin and all the gods, and thereupon set fire to the whole world.

Thor, was the god of thunder and strength : with his hammer he slew Yults, Trolds, and other foes of Odin and the gods.

Tyr, one of the bravest and wisest gods, so that it was customary to say proverbially, "As bold as Tyr," "Wise as Tyr."

Valfather, the father of the slain or fallen in battle : one of Odin's surnames.

Valhall (*the Hall of the Slain*), the place where all warriors who had fallen by the enemy were so nobly entertained by Odin. It is commonly called Valhalla; but Valhall is the right, and *Valhalla* only the Latinized name in Resenius' edition of the Edda.

Valkyrier, were virgins, or war-maids, who waited upon the heroes in Valhall. Three of them, amongst whom was Rota, were commonly dispatched to the field of battle by Odin, in order to choose them who were to be slain, which employment the name Valkyrier denotes. These three have obtained a place in this tragedy, and Rota is made the principal of them.

Udgaard (Udgard), Loke's dwelling outside of heaven. His usual name in the Edda is Udgarda Loke, Loke of Udgard ; and thus Saxo in the Life of Gorm the first calls him Ugartilocum.

Ymer, the first giant, Yutt, or Jotun, who lived before the heaven and the earth existed, and who was killed with all his offspring by Odin and his brothers. Only one of this giant race, by name Borgeline, escaped, together with his wife, and became the stem-father of the subsequent Jotuns.

PRINTED BY BALLANTYNE, HANSON AND CO.
LONDON AND EDINBURGH

www.ingramcontent.com/pod-product-compliance
Lightning Source LLC
Chambersburg PA
CBHW032358020726
47499CB00008B/2802